Enid Blyton's
NODDY
and the Milkman

BBC CHILDREN'S BOOKS

Bumpy Dog was staying with Noddy while Tessie Bear
visited her aunt. It was breakfast time and he had just
drunk the last of Noddy's milk.

"Let's go and see where Mr Milko is," said Noddy. "He's never usually this late. I wonder what can be the matter?"

Bumpy Dog was wagging his tail. He could hear Mr Milko outside.

"Milk-o, milk-oooh!" shouted Mr Milko, as Bumpy Dog jumped up and knocked him over. Noddy's milk went flying into the air.

"Oh, Bumpy Dog!" cried Noddy, diving to catch his bottle of milk. "I am sorry, Mr Milko. Bumpy Dog can be very naughty sometimes."

"I'm sorry too, Noddy," said Mr Milko. "I'm sorry I'm late, but I am worried about my brother. He is not very well, so I must go and see him. But I can't take a day off from my milk round."

"I will do your milk round for you tomorrow!" said Noddy happily. "I'd love to be a milkman."

But just then, they heard a loud crash.

Bumpy Dog had knocked one of the wheels off
Mr Milko's cart!

"Oh no! I shan't even be able to deliver the milk today!"
cried Mr Milko.

"We can deliver the milk in my little car," said Noddy.
"We'll mend the cart when we get back."

Noddy and Mr Milko arrived at Pink Cat's house.
"I'm sorry that I'm late," said Mr Milko.
"I should think you are," scolded Pink Cat. "I'm having my whiskers curled this morning, and you have made me late. I shall have to rush."

"I'm not going to pay you your two pennies today, milkman. I shall give them to you tomorrow – if you are on time, and if you leave that naughty dog at home." Pink Cat walked crossly back to her house.

"Don't worry, Mr Milko," said Noddy. "I shall collect the money tomorrow."

Noddy and Mr Milko drove off quickly to deliver
Bert Monkey's milk. He was chatting to Dinah Doll,
waiting for the milkman.

"There you are at last!" said Bert Monkey. "I thought you weren't coming today!"

"I'm sorry I'm late," said Mr Milko, giving Bert Monkey his milk.

But Bumpy Dog thought that Bert's naughty tail was stealing the milk.

Bumpy Dog jumped up at Bert Monkey and knocked the milk right out of his tail!

"Stop it, Bumpy!" cried Noddy. "Bert Monkey is not stealing the milk. He is going to pay for it."

"No, I'm not! It's smashed!" said Bert Monkey. "I shall take another bottle and pay you tomorrow, when that naughty dog has gone!"

Noddy and Mr Milko drove back to Noddy's house to mend the milk cart.

"Do you really think you can do my milk round, Noddy?" asked Mr Milko.

"Oh yes! Oh yes, please!" said Noddy.

"But you mustn't let Bumpy Dog come with you," warned Mr Milko.

"I shan't, I promise!" said Noddy.

Mr Tubby Bear was helping to mend the cart.
"Thank you very much," said Mr Milko. "I just need my
spanner to tighten up the wheel." Mr Milko looked all
around him. "Where is my spanner?"

"Oh, Bumpy Dog!" said Noddy. "Bring that spanner back here." But Bumpy Dog would not come back.

"Don't worry, Noddy," said Mr Tubby Bear. "I'll find the spanner. Take Mr Milko to the station now, and I'll tighten the wheel."

When Noddy came back from the station, Mr Tubby Bear had finished mending the wheel.

"Bumpy Dog was trying to hide the spanner in my garden," he said. "He really can be naughty! I shall look after him tomorrow for you, Noddy. I shan't let him out until you have delivered all the milk."

"Oh, thank you very much, Mr Tubby Bear! Bumpy, you must be a good dog!" said Noddy.

Noddy was up very early the next morning to deliver the milk. He drove his little car to Pink Cat's house and took the milk up to her door.

"Hello, Noddy. Where is the milkman?" asked Pink Cat.

"I am the milkman today, and you owe me four pence, please!" said Noddy.

"Here you are," said Pink Cat. "You are a very good milkman. You are not even late! You can collect the empty bottles from my doorstep."

Noddy went to Pink Cat's house to pick up her
empty bottles.

"Woof, woof!" It was Bumpy Dog, followed by
Mr Tubby Bear. Bumpy was so pleased to see Noddy
that he knocked the empty bottles right off the
doorstep and away down the street.

"Oh, no! Bumpy Dog, what are you doing here?"
cried Noddy.

But Bumpy Dog had run away again. He was chasing
the empty milk bottles.

The bottles went rolling down the street, past Mr Sparks' garage. Bumpy Dog was running after them. Noddy and Mr Tubby Bear were running after Bumpy Dog.

Bumpy Dog jumped onto Mr Sparks' trolley, and shot off down the street.

"Where are you going with my trolley?" cried Mr Sparks. "Oh, good heavens! What is happening?"

Noddy and Mr Tubby Bear ran past, still chasing naughty Bumpy Dog. "Come back! Come back at once, Bumpy Dog," they shouted.

"Don't worry, Mr Sparks," added Noddy, hastily. "Your milk will soon be here. Come back, Bumpy!"

But Bumpy Dog was enjoying himself. He raced through Toy Town, and nearly knocked over Mr Wobbly Man, the Clockwork Mouse and Mr Plod. Mr Plod looked very cross indeed.

Bumpy Dog didn't stop until he bumped into Dinah Doll's stall.

"What are you doing?" asked Dinah Doll.

"Woof, woof!" barked Bumpy.

"You *are* excited," said Dinah Doll. "This bone will calm you down. Oh, hello, Noddy. Hello, Mr Tubby Bear." Noddy and Mr Tubby Bear could not believe their eyes. Bumpy Dog was being good at last!

"Thank you very much, Dinah," said Noddy.
"You're very kind. I can go and rescue Pink Cat's
empty bottles now."

Noddy followed the two bottles, which had rolled down to the police station.

"Oh, there you are!" he cried, and went to pick them up.

"Two pints, please," said Sly the goblin.

"Hello, Noddy," said Mr Plod. "I heard that you were the milkman today. I caught these two bad goblins stealing cakes last night, so I shall need two extra pints of milk. Here are two extra pennies for you."

"Thank you, Mr Plod. Two extra pennies! Mr Milko will think I'm a very good milkman, after all."

At last, it was time to pick up Tessie Bear and Mr Milko.
"Hello!" shouted Noddy. "Do get in.
I have come to drive you both home.
And look, here are two extra pennies
for you, Mr Milko!"

"Well done, Noddy!" said Mr Milko happily.
"What a good milkman you are. I am so pleased,
I shall just have to ring your little bell!"
   And he did!

Other Noddy *TV Tie-in titles*
available from BBC Children's Books

Published by BBC Books
a division of BBC Enterprises Limited
Woodlands, 80 Wood Lane, London W12 0TT
First published 1993
Text and stills copyright © BBC Enterprises Limited 1993
ISBN 0 563 36863 2

Based on the Television series, produced by Cosgrove Hall Productions, inspired by the Noddy Books
which are copyright © Darrell Waters Limited 1949-1968

Enid Blyton's signature and Noddy are Trademarks of Darrell Waters Limited

Typeset in 17/21 pt Garamond by BBC Books

Printed and bound in Great Britain by Cambus Limited, East Kilbride
Colour separations by DOT Gradations, Chelmsford
Cover printed by Cambus Limited, East Kilbride